I0583738

You're Only a Top?

The Dr. Cage Chronicles: Memoirs of a Sex Therapist

You're Only a Top?

GRAYSON ACE

4 Horsemen
Publications, Inc.

4 Horsemen
Publications, Inc.

4 Horsemen Publications, Inc.
1497 Main St. Suite 169
Dunedin, FL 34698
4horsemenpublications.com
info@4horsemenpublications.com

Cover & Typesetting by Battle Goddess Productions
Editor Tilda M. Cooke

Paperback ISBN-13: 978-1-64450-109-2
Ebook ISBN-13: 978-1-64450-108-5

This book is dedicated to everyone who stood
behind me through some of the most trying
times of my life.

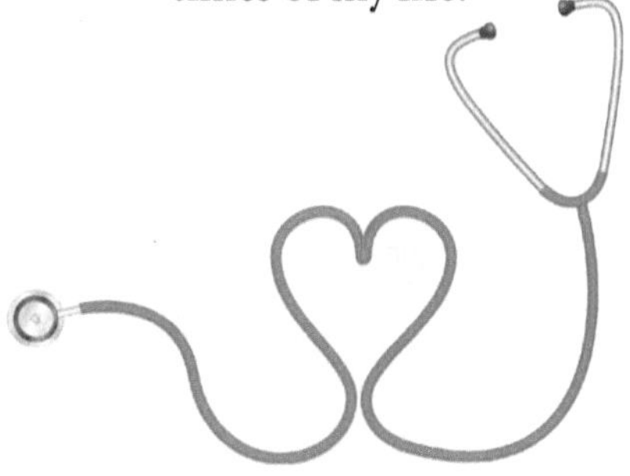

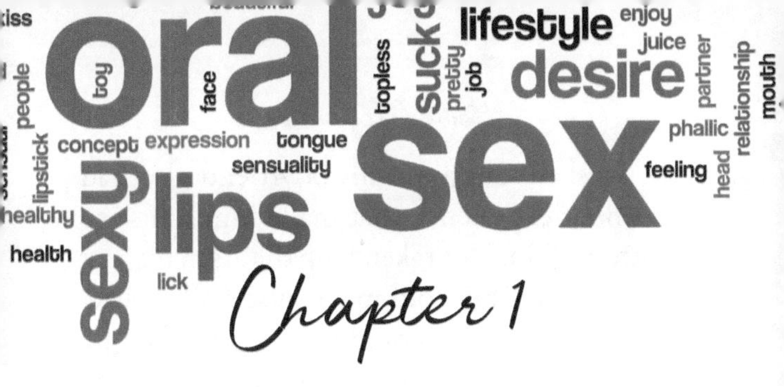

Chapter 1

CHARLIE:
THE TOTAL TOP

"I just don't like anything going up my butt. When I was younger, my finger ripped through the toilet paper and went into my hole, and it hurt really bad. Ever since that day, I knew I was never even going to try putting anything up there because I knew it wouldn't feel good." That was Charlie's response when I asked what he meant by "I'm only a top." I was a bit blown away by his reasoning, but to each his own.

I asked Charlie if his boyfriend also had a similar experience that made him refuse to bottom. "No. He's taken it up the ass in his past relationships but told me he just really wasn't into it. He said he could never cum when he was bottoming, so one day he just decided he was never going to try it again."

In order to better understand what I was dealing with, I needed to know more about how they coped with their sex lives, and what their sex life was actually like. All the while, I couldn't help but wonder how they could go this long without taking it up the ass.

I asked Charlie to tell me about his last sex session with his boyfriend and told him I needed him to include every single detail as if he were writing his story in a book. Charlie began to tell me what their typical intimate interactions were like with each other.

My boyfriend's name is Dante. We've never had full intercourse with each other since we're both tops, so everything we do is just foreplay. Two nights ago was the last time we were intimate with each other.

I had a long tiring day at work, and I showered as soon as I got home, just as I always do. When I got out of the shower and walked back into the bedroom, Dante was lying on the bed, naked, stroking his already hard cock. He looked at me, smiled, and motioned for me to come over toward him. I dropped my towel and walked over toward the bed. As I got closer to the bed, Dante rolled over to the side and grabbed my hips, pulling me closer to his face. He put my soft dick in his mouth and started sucking on it. I could feel him rolling his tongue around the head while he bobbed up and down on my shaft.

Within a minute, I was fully hard, and he was struggling to get my entire cock in his mouth. He rolled onto his back with his head leaning off the bed so I could fuck his face, and he started stroking on his own dick. I began thrusting my hips, forcing my hard piece in and out of his mouth, and then bent forward so I could start sucking on his cock. His dick is about the same size as mine, but I have no problems getting the whole thing in my mouth. I kept thrusting my hips and fucking his mouth while I was sucking on his throbbing dick, and even started sucking on his balls a little bit. Dante loves when I suck on his balls and stroke his cock, and he started letting out some deep moans while I was doing this.

I stood up so that I could get on the bed and grabbed his shoulders to roll him up toward the pillows. I laid with my body on top of his, grabbed his face, and started kissing him. We made out for a good ten or fifteen minutes, grinding our cocks together and Dante occasionally slapping my ass. I began kissing his neck and started kissing my way back down toward his dick. There was pre-cum dripping all out of his cock, but I quickly licked it all up. I moved down toward his balls and sucked on them for a few minutes while I was stroking his cock. I could see Dante clench on to the sheets and thrust his hips up toward the ceiling in pure pleasure. He likes getting his balls sucked on more than his dick.

I grabbed the back of his knees and pushed his legs into the air. My tongue slowly went from his balls down to his beautiful hole. Even though he won't bottom, he still loves getting his ass rimmed. I slowly licked around his hole and gently over the top of it before spreading his cheeks so I could get my tongue deep inside of him. Dante grabbed onto his cock and started stroking it, and I knew this was how he wanted to blow his load. I kept thrusting my tongue in and out of his hole like I was fucking him. After all, it's the closest I was going to get to being inside of him.

Within a few minutes, he told me he was going to cum, and I quickly pulled out of his ass and let his legs down so I could get my face up toward his cock. I wanted him to shoot his load all over my face. Dante kept stroking his cock while I rubbed his balls, and almost instantly started shooting his load all over the mouth and the side of my face. His cum shoots out almost in streams, and his cumshots can last for several seconds. I opened my mouth so the cum would shoot inside, and when he was done, I started sucking on his dick again to get every last drop.

Dante grabbed my head and pulled me up toward his so he could start kissing me again. He licked some of the cum off the side of my face and stuck his cum covered tongue in my mouth to make out. We're both a bit of cum whores, so this kind of stuff turns us on even more. After a few minutes of making out and getting cum all over, he laid down flat on the bed so I could fuck his face again.

I quickly moved my cock up toward his willing mouth and shoved it all the way in, making him gag a little bit. I pulled my cock out and bent down so I could spit in his mouth, and then shoved my cock back in. He didn't have time to swallow the spit, so I could feel my dick slide down his throat just a little bit easier. His mouth is like a vacuum, and it only took about 30 seconds of fucking his face before I was blowing my load down his throat. He enjoys swallowing more, and I like having the cum on my face more.

He sucked up every last bit of cum until there was nothing left coming out of my cock. I leaned down and gave him a kiss, said "good game," and then turned the TV on so we could watch Real Housewives.

And that's it. That's pretty much what every intimate interaction is like between us. Well, that is, unless we invite someone else to join us.

And with that statement I told Charlie that his time was up, but that I wanted him to schedule another session so we could get into more details about their sex life involving others. Charlie smiled and scheduled a session for the next day. I would normally get up and walk my patients out of my office, but with the massive boner I had, I felt it was best to just stay in my seat.

Chapter 2

RASHID

After hearing Charlie's story, I was pretty horned up and needed to get some action soon. I pulled out my phone and logged into my apps, but this time, I was looking for something different. In order to better understand who Charlie was, I needed to find myself a total top. So, in reality, this hook-up was going to be research. Okay, I say that now. In reality, this hook-up was so I could get a nut, and maybe ask some questions, too.

I started reading different profiles, only looking at the ones that just said "top." Most people tend to put versatile, but in all honesty, most of them are total bottoms. After a few minutes, I stumbled upon Rashid's profile. He was my age and looked to be Italian with maybe a little Middle Eastern in him. He was extremely handsome, had dark features, and was pretty well built. In his profile, he specifically wrote that he was a "total top," so I was really hoping that he would respond. Not even 30 seconds passed after I messaged him before he replied.

We made small talk for a little bit and then he asked what I was looking for. I was honest and told him that I was all horned up and wanted to fuck. He sent me a picture of his cock – rock hard, slightly hairy base, and a thick nine inches. This was going to be fun. He asked if he could fuck me raw, and of course, I wasn't going to deny that. I was hoping that he'd want to come over after I left the office, but he said he preferred morning sex and wanted to pick me up and take me for coffee first. I thought that was a little weird, and told him I didn't even drink coffee, but agreed to the "date." I told him to text me in the morning, and I'd give him my address.

Charlie was my only patient of the day, and there was no point in hanging around the office, so I started packing up my things. I was still a bit horny from listening to his story and thinking about the dick I was going to get in the morning. I was about to walk out of the office but decided to have a quick jerk off session before I headed home. I set my bag down on the desk, took a seat on the lounge in the reception area and whipped my dick out. I didn't even pull up any porn on my phone – I just kept visualizing Charlie and Dante going at it, and me offering up my ass to help them out. It didn't take long, and within 30 seconds, I was shooting my load on the couch. I cleaned up, grabbed my things, and headed home.

My phone started going off around 6:30 the next morning. It was Rashid, and I was actually a little pissed that he was messaging me that early. He asked for my address and said he was on his way over. I didn't even have time to shower, so I threw on some clothes, brushed my teeth, and cleaned my junk with a wet washcloth. He texted me when he was outside, and I ran downstairs and jumped into his Benz.

Rashid immediately looked at me and told me what a beautiful man I was, and he leaned over and gave me a kiss like he was picking up his boyfriend. He started to drive and said this was like our first date. After driving around the block twice, he parked his car and asked if he could come up and see my place. I'm not sure why he asked because we had already established that we were fucking.

We walked upstairs, and I gave him a little tour of the apartment. Luckily Jackie was gone, so I didn't need to worry about her hearing or walking in on us. Rashid asked if he could see my bedroom, and as soon as we walked in, he grabbed me and turned me around so he could start kissing me. I backed up to the bed while he was kissing me and sat down on the edge, continuing to make out with him. He was in gym shorts, and I quickly started pulling them down so I could release that monster cock of his – he proved to be a grower *and* a shower.

I grabbed onto his cock while still kissing him and started stroking it. Rashid put his hand on my head and pushed me down toward his cock, and it was obvious what he wanted. I lifted his dick up so I could start with his balls and started licking under his balls and up to the shaft. I went down farther under his balls toward his hole to see what he would do, and just like I thought he grabbed my head and steered me back up toward his cock – he didn't want me going near his hole.

He pushed my head back against the side of my bed so I really couldn't move it and started fucking my mouth. He pushed his cock in and out pretty quickly, and I started jerking on my hard dick. After a few minutes he pulled his cock out and hopped on the bed. I wiped off my mouth and got up on the bed and strattled him so I could get my dick in his mouth.

I started moving my way up and aimed my dick for his mouth, but instead he grabbed underneath my legs and propped my whole body up so that my ass was in his face. Does this guy not like sucking dick? I was about to say something and then I felt his tongue slide right into my hole. I definitely wasn't prepared to get rimmed – he didn't give me a chance to shower before he came over. That didn't stop him. He slid his tongue up and down my crack and I could feel him spreading my ass with his hands so he could get in deep. He was really good with his tongue, and I thought he was going to make me cum.

I let him lick my hole for a good ten minutes, but then I couldn't take it anymore because I was afraid I was going to shoot my load and not get to fuck. I grabbed the lube and the poppers and started getting his dick nice and ready. He took a hit of the poppers first, and then I did before sliding his huge cock in my ass. I told him that my riding him was going to be the only position because of how big he was, and he was totally fine with that.

I slowly sat down on his cock, and I could just feel him stretching my hole out. I'm used to being a bottom, but this one took some getting used to, even more than when I let Juan fuck me. Once my hole completely devoured his cock, I sat there for a minute to just let things down below get better acquainted. He leaned forward and started kissing me, and then grabbed onto my hips and made my body start moving. His dick inside of me felt amazing, and feeling it thrust in and out made my cock get rock hard.

I bounced up and down on his tool, leaning down to kiss him and pinching his nipples a bit. I leaned back and started rubbing his balls, hoping it would make him cum. I started moving my finger down toward his hole, but he quickly swatted it away, just as I thought.

As I was moving up and down on his cock, my balls were rubbing pretty hard on his chest, and I knew I was going to cum without having to even touch myself. I didn't want it to end, but I knew I couldn't hold it much longer. I screamed, "I'm going to cum," and my load shot straight above his head and above the headboard onto the wall. I must have let out the loudest moan I had ever let out in my life.

Rashid looked at me and smiled, and then said, "Yeah, I'm that good." I'm not really sure if anyone had ever made me cum without touching myself, but I was pretty impressed. I leaned down and kissed him, and he started thrusting his dick in and out of my hole. I'm not about that, at all, and quickly hopped off. He seemed a bit upset, but I told him once I cum, I physically can't have anything inside my ass – the intensity is way too much.

He pulled me over and started making out with me while he started stroking his cock. I wasn't in the mood to make out at that point

– I needed to get in the shower. But it was only fair that he got to shoot his load too. I played with his nipples a little bit, and then went down and started grabbing his balls. I didn't even try to go for his hole this time because I learned that was a no-no. He said he was going to cum, and he turned over so he could shoot his load on my chest. He had a pretty good shot and let out a few loud moans.

Once he was finished spraying his baby batter all over my chest, he ran his finger up through it and put it in my mouth. I had no intentions on letting him get cum in my mouth, but at this point, whatever. He asked if he could shower, and I pointed at the bathroom as I lie there, covered in his splooge. He got out of the shower, still smiling, and said he'd come back and fuck my "man pussy" anytime I wanted him to. I'd probably call him again because it was a pretty good fuck, even if he wouldn't suck my dick.

He kept talking about my hole, and saying how it was his, and kept referring to it as a pussy. At this point, I just wanted to get in the shower, so I told him that I was going to be late for a patient. He left, and I finally understood what Charlie was going through just a little bit better.

Chapter 3

CHARLIE'S THREESOME

I looked at my watch and realized I was going to be super late getting into the office, so I showered as fast as I could and bolted out the door. I couldn't remember what time Charlie's appointment was, but I didn't want to risk missing it. After all, he was the only patient that I had!

I got to the office and looked at my calendar, and of course I had two hours before Charlie's appointment. I logged onto my computer to check the message system, and I couldn't believe what I was seeing – I had requests from five different men for appointments! I wasn't exactly sure how this happened or who was blessing me with these appointments, but I could only assume Charlie must have told some of his friends. Regardless, this was exactly what I needed to get the momentum going!

Just as I was contacting the last person on the list who requested an appointment, Charlie walked in the door. As a therapist, it's always nice to see your patients coming back because it means that they see the value in what you're helping them with. With a giant smile he greeted me, and I told him to go get comfortable in my office while I finished up the schedule.

I apologized for running a bit late, but Charlie didn't seem bothered by it. He told me that he spoke about his session with a few of his friends, which is exactly what I thought had happened. I thanked him for the referrals and told him if he could get five more to schedule with me that I would give him a referral discount.

I wanted to get right into the session and speak more about Charlie's and Dante's sex life. I repeated a summary version of what Charlie had told me during our previous session and asked Charlie if oral sex is the only type of intimacy that he and Dante have with each other. Charlie let out a big laugh and responded, "Oh Lord, no. Do you really think we're going to go without fucking? We invite other guys who we know are bottoms to join us all the time."

I already knew that they had threesomes because I had seen Charlie's profile on one of my apps, but naturally I couldn't insinuate this. I told Charlie that, just like our previous session, I needed him to tell me about the last time that he and Dante invited someone else to join them for sex, not leaving out any details. Charlie, of course, was more than happy to share, and adjusted himself in his chair, kind of like, "I hope you're ready for this."

Last weekend, Dante and I went out to the club, specifically looking for someone to bring home. We had both been pretty horny, and this is typically what we do when we want to fuck. We either go on the apps and find someone, or we meet a cute guy at the club. The club was doing a special for all the local colleges, so we knew we could easily find some hot little jock with a nice round ass.

We would talk to a few guys, and then once one really sparked our interest we would start flirting, buy him a few drinks, and then ask if he wanted to come back and fuck. We always made things very clear – that we were both tops and that we had every intention of fucking him. This guy's name was Mark. He was 23, just graduated from college, and played on the football team. He had an almost perfect plump ass, but not as plump as yours.

I looked up from my tablet when he said this and just grinned a little bit. Charlie gave me a look I had seen before, but I brushed it off and told him to continue.

Mark. Yeah. He was fucking hot. He had huge biceps and you could tell he had an amazing chest. We left the bar and took the train back to our place, and I just remember wondering what his cock looked like the entire way back.

When we got home, Dante went into the kitchen to make a few drinks, but I wasted no time getting started on Mark. I sat down on the couch and pulled Mark over toward me and had him straddle my lap. I pulled his head toward mine and started making out with him. He was a really great kisser, and we immediately pulled each other's shirts off. Mark started kissing and sucking on my neck, and then kissed his way to my nipples. He bit them a little and then made his way down my chest toward my dick. He looked up at me and was kissing my stomach while he was rubbing his hand on my dick through my pants.

Mark started unbuttoning my jeans and opened them just enough to pull my dick out. I was semi-hard at this point, and Mark started slowly licking the head of my penis. He would lick the tip of it, then twirl his tongue around it a little bit before finally swallowing the entire thing. Just as he started sucking on it, Dante walked in from the kitchen. He sat down next to me with his drink and put his hand on the back of Mark's head as he bobbed up and down on my tool. Dante always likes watching me get pleasured for a little bit before joining in.

Dante leaned over and started kissing me, and after a few minutes, Mark moved over to start working on his dick. Dante leaned back on the couch and put his hands behind his head, letting Mark do all the work. Mark completely pulled Dante's shorts off, exposing his rock-solid dick. He wasn't gentle with it like he was with mine, and he just went to town on him. Dante was letting out some pretty big moans, and I leaned over and pulled Dante's shirt off and started sucking on his nipples.

When I saw Mark get up off his knees and more into the doggy position, I knew I needed to get behind him. I pulled his shorts and briefs off of him, exposing that perfect round ass. He had absolutely no body hair, and his hole was pristine. I spit on my hand to get my finger wet and started rubbing in on his hole. He never even flinched and kept sucking on Dante's cock. I leaned forward and slowly started to kiss his cheeks before rolling my tongue into his tight hole. Just as I did this, he arched his back like a cat, and I knew he liked it.

I buried my face as deep in his ass as I could for a few more minutes before Dante said he wanted to taste it. He pulled Mark up on the couch so that he was standing over Dante and kind of crouching down with his ass in Dante's face. I could see his long tongue going right into Mark's ass. Dante's cock was kind of bouncing around while he was eating Mark's ass, so I crawled forward and grabbed a hold of it and started sucking on the head like a fish. I was stroking it while I was sucking it because I knew that's exactly how Dante liked it. In between tongue thrusts, I could hear both Dante and Mark letting out loud moans.

This went on for a few more minutes before Dante told Mark it was time to sit on his dick. I got up to go grab the lube, but when I came back into the living room, Mark was already riding him. Dante must have really gotten his hole soaking wet. He was riding Dante's cock with his knees bent and only his feet holding him up, and Dante was grabbing onto his ass to kind of assist. I pulled my pants the rest of the way off and stood over Dante facing Mark so that he could suck my cock. Mark grabbed onto my dick and shoved it into his mouth, and then I felt Dante's tongue slip into my hole. I had one hand on the back of Mark's head while it bobbed back and forth on my wet dick, and my other hand on the back of Dante's head pulling his face closer into my ass.

I wanted to get a piece of Mark's ass, so I said it was my turn and hopped off the couch. I went behind Mark and kind of pulled him off of Mark's cock and pushed him forward a little bit, so he was leaning over Dante's shoulder. Dante grabbed Mark's ass and spread it open for me while I lubed up my cock, and that thing slid right into Mark's loose hole. I grabbed onto his hips and fucked him as hard as I could, and I could tell he liked it. Dante was kissing Mark's shoulder and neck, and I could see him reaching down and grabbing for Mark's cock to jerk him off. Fucking a hole after Dante always kind of sucked because it was always super loose.

I fucked him for a few more minutes before saying it was time to DP. I pulled out of his hole so that he could sit back on Dante's dick, which slid in with no problem. Mark started bouncing up and down, and while he did, I poured lube down his crack and pushed it into his hole with my finger. I put extra lube on my cock and pressed the head of it against Mark's hole, just above

Dante's cock. I was able to get the head in with no problem, and Mark was moaning louder than I had heard earlier. I let the head sit there for a minute, and when Mark started moving his ass back and forth a little bit, I started pushing more of my rod into his ass.

It took a few minutes, but my entire shaft was all the way in his hole with Dante's. I thrust just a little bit because I knew between the friction of our dicks inside his ass, that I was going to blow my load pretty quickly. Mark arched his back and leaned toward me so he could kiss me, and Dante leaned forward and started kissing his chest. Not much time had passed, and I started blowing my load deep in his hole. Just as I did, I could feel Dante's cock start to throb, and I knew he was blowing his load too. That, and he let out his loud orgasmic screech. We both pumped our cum deep into Mark's hole, and then I slowly pulled my cock out before Dante did. When my dick popped out, so did a shit ton of cum.

Mark got off of Dante's dick and sat next to him on the couch and started stroking his dick. I knelt down in front of him and stuck a few fingers in his ass to help and started sucking on his balls. Dante leaned down and started sucking on his shaft, and not even ten seconds later Mark yelled out that he was going to cum. We let Mark grab his dick and stroke his load out, both of us eagerly waiting to catch his warm load in our mouths.

This kid could shoot a fucking load like no other. He got so much in my mouth that I actually had to close it so I didn't gag, and he still covered half my face. Same with Dante. Dante turned to me and started making out with me, and it was like getting a second load to the face. I swallowed what was in my mouth and wiped off with a towel. I told Mark he could shower if he wanted, but he said he wanted to keep our loads in his ass as long as he could. He left, and then Dante and I jumped into the shower and went to bed.

At some point during Charlie's story, I stopped taking notes and just started fantasizing about being Mark, in the middle of these two gorgeous men. I told Charlie that I needed some time to process everything to come up with a proper treatment plan, and that I wanted him to bring Dante with him for his next session, so we could get his point of view. Charlie made his appointment for the next day, and I knew exactly what course of treatment was going to have to happen.

Chapter 4

CHRIS

*H*earing about Charlie's and Dante's threesome with Mark brought up a lot of memories from when Thomas and I would invite others to play with us. I tried to forget about all the threesomes and foursomes we had because it was a somewhat dark part of my life – realizing I was with someone who was so addicted to sex and that was the reason why he wanted us to invite others into our bedroom.

I packed up my stuff to head home, but then I sat down on the couch and started scrolling through old photos on my phone. Thomas and I had been broken up for about a year, but I still thought about him a lot, and even though I always felt disgusting after our group activities, they sure as fuck were hot when they were happening.

The first threesome we ever had was with a guy named Chris. Thomas and I would go to this one restaurant at least once a week, and Chris always seemed to be our waiter. We kind of got to know each other, and it was obvious that he was gay. He was tall and muscular with blonde hair and a super cute smile. He was pretty flamboyant acting, so it was a total surprise when he ended up telling us he was a total top. Thomas, I would say, was a 90% top. He never wanted to let me stick it in him, unless it was me being woken up at 2:30 in the morning by him sucking my dick and then getting on top of it. Other than that, he was the top in the relationship. So it always pissed me off when we were with other guys and he would bottom for them.

We ended up running into Chris at the bar one night, and he immediately started buying us drinks and was super flirtatious. He almost seemed to be looking for an excuse to put his hands on one of us. We went to the dance floor and started dancing with each other – I started making out with Thomas, and before I knew it, Chris grabbed me and shoved his tongue down my throat, and then turned to Thomas and did the same thing. He grabbed both of our dicks and said he wanted to go back to our place.

It was pretty obvious what was going to happen. I hopped in the driver seat to get us home. As soon as we pulled out of the parking lot, Thomas leaned over and unzipped my pants and started sucking my dick. Chris was in the backseat and leaned forward, shoving Thomas's head down on my dick. He whipped his own dick out and started stroking on it. I could see it in the rearview mirror, and it was pretty massive. I pulled Thomas's head off my cock because he was close to making me cum, and I wanted to save it for when we got home.

We walked into the house, and all of us immediately took off all our clothes. I hopped on the bed first and Chris jumped on top of me and started kissing me, grinding his cock on mine. Thomas went up behind Chris and started licking his hole. With every lick Thomas made, Chris would grind his cock harder against mine. Thomas pulled Chris off of me and went down and started sucking my cock, and Chris went behind him and shoved his tongue right into his hole.

Before I knew it, I saw Chris spit on his hand to lube up his dick, and he was shoving it in Thomas's hole. For someone who never really bottomed, Thomas sure took Chris's dick pretty easily. Thomas quickly picked my legs up and pinned them back on the bed and scooted up to slide his cock into my ass. This was the first time I was experiencing something like this. With every thrust Chris made into

Thomas, I could feel it relaying through his cock into my hole.

After a few minutes, I said I wanted to take Chris's cock, and Thomas pulled out of me and got in front of me on all fours. I lubed up Chris's dick because I wasn't about to take it with just spit. I stuck my tongue in Thomas's hole to get it wet and then slipped my tool inside his loose hole. Chris came up behind me and put his in pretty slowly because he knew it was going to take a minute. This was one of the best feelings I had ever experienced and was something I had always thought about – fucking and getting fucked at the same time.

We fucked like this for about five or six minutes when Thomas started begging to fuck Chris. Chris was hesitant, but told Thomas to eat his ass first, and then take it from there. Chris pulled his dick out of me, but I kept fucking Thomas because his hole was finally forming to my cock. Chris got in front of me and sat on Thomas's face, facing me, and we started making out. He was letting out some pretty loud moans, obviously enjoying what was going on.

I was still pounding away at Thomas's ass when Chris stood up from his face and turned around. He lubed up Thomas's dick and slowly started to sit down on it and let it slide in his ass. I was still fucking Thomas and kind of laughed and made a comment about him being a top. Chris said he only says that to avoid having to bottom if he doesn't feel like it. He took Thomas's cock pretty easily and started bouncing up and down on it while I was thrusting mine deep into Thomas's ass. It didn't take long before Thomas said he was going to cum, and he pumped his load deep in Chris's ass.

Once I could tell Thomas was done shooting his load, I pushed Chris up off Thomas's dick so I could fuck him. I put a little more lube on my cock and shoved it right into Chris's ass. There was already some cum starting to drip out, so that helped my cock ease into it. I didn't even have to do much work because Chris was bouncing his ass back and forth on my rod. He leaned forward and was making out with Thomas while I pounded away.

I could tell I was going to cum and didn't even give any warning. I thrust my dick as hard as I could to shoot my load and let out a loud scream of relief. I pushed it in a few more times to make sure my dick was fully drained and then pulled my cock out and pushed Chris over on his back. I started sucking on Chris's dick, and Thomas got up to join me. Within minutes, Chris was shooting his load all on the sides of our faces, and we were doing everything we could to get it into our mouths. I licked some of the cum off of Thomas's cheek and then leaned down to make out with Chris and put it into his mouth.

We rolled around with each other for a little while longer, making out and rubbing our hands all over one another. We showered, and Chris ended up staying the night, sleeping in between us and cuddling. At one point I woke up and noticed the blanket moving up and down, and realized it was Thomas's head swallowing Chris's dick. At this point, I was too exhausted to join in, so I just pretended I didn't see it.

I drove Chris home the next day because Thomas had to go to work. But don't you know that asshole made me stay on the phone with him the entire time I was in the car with Chris? He knew what he had done while I was sleeping, and naturally thought that I would do the same. Well guess what? I did.

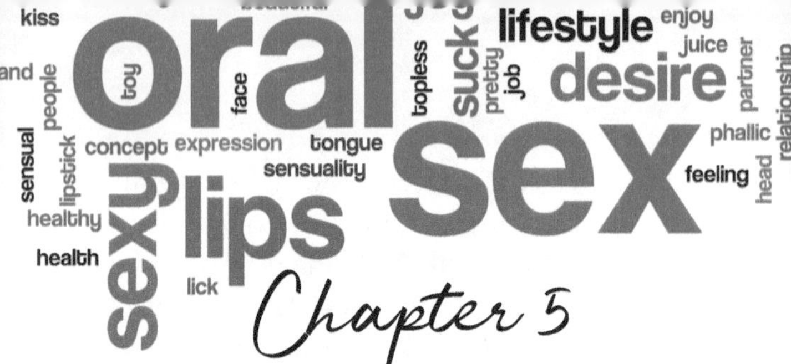

Chapter 5

BRANDON & MICHAEL

*S*ince we're on the topic of my sexcapades while dating Thomas, Chris definitely wasn't the only guy we invited into our bedroom. Looking back, there were actually several guys that we messed around with together, some of which Thomas fucked around with behind my back.

There was Eric, whom I had actually messed around with before I met Thomas. He was in love with me, so when I started dating Thomas, I took him over there, and he watched while Thomas fucked me. Through Eric, we met an older couple who lived across the street from him. We ended up having several foursomes with them, and even had just one of them over once. After the fact, I found out that the one we had over by himself – Thomas would then fuck him behind my back. Karma, I guess. There was obviously Chris from the restaurant. And there was Nathan, a guy we met at a bar while on a trip to Nashville for a wedding. We brought Nathan back to our hotel room, which we were sharing with another couple, and fucked out on the balcony. This was actually my first time participating in a train, with Thomas fucking Nathan while Nathan fucked me. I tried looking Nathan up after Thomas and I broke up but didn't have any luck.

Then there was Brandon and Michael. Brandon and I actually went to college together and had a few classes with each other, but we really didn't talk much. I remember him telling me he always wondered if I was gay and wished he would have made a move on me in college. I wished he would have, too. He was super cute, kind of looked like me, and had a really nice cock. Brandon was the GM at a restaurant that I frequented, and we ended up exchanging numbers just on a friendly basis.

I knew Brandon had a boyfriend and was hoping this would become more of a double dating situation. The four of us hung out quite frequently. We would go out to eat, go bowling, and sometimes go to each other's house for dinner and a movie. One night, we invited Michael and Brandon over to watch a movie, and we moved the couches in front of the TV, so we could all sit together.

We started the movie, and Michael put his arm around me while Brandon put his arm around Thomas. I turned and looked over and noticed Thomas's hand rubbing over the top of Brandon's dick, so I figured what the hell. I turned to Michael and started making out with him. I had wanted this for a while and was already hard thinking about what was going to happen. I could see that Thomas and

Brandon were already going at it on the other end of the couch, but I really didn't pay too much attention.

I got up from the couch and grabbed Michael's hand and led him into my bedroom. I wasn't really sure what I was doing – Thomas and I had never separated during a hookup. When I went into the bedroom, I saw Thomas and Brandon get up from the couch and go into the spare bedroom. I didn't really like this, but I started it. They were obviously going to fuck, and so was I. I was just hoping that Thomas wasn't going to let Brandon top him.

I pushed Michael down onto the bed and pulled his shorts off. His huge cock flung back up after it bounced off his briefs. I immediately swallowed his entire cock, making me gag as it went down my throat. It wasn't super thick, but it was a solid eight inches. He grabbed onto the back of my head and started moving his hips up and down to make his cock go in and out of my mouth. I came up for some air and moved up to him and started kissing him. He would kiss my neck and then move back to my lips, rubbing his hands all over my back and pulling my shirt off. I quickly pulled my shorts down and moved up so I could shove my dick in his mouth. He grabbed onto my cock and started stroking it while he was sucking on it, and I reached back and stroked his piece.

I told him I wanted to fuck him and grabbed the lube and started lubing his dick up, but he told me I needed to get a condom. I fucking hate using condoms, but I wanted his cock and needed to respect that. Thomas and I kept condoms in the drawer for things like this, and you know for damn sure I kept a count on them so I would know if Thomas used one without me. Michael put the condom on and lubed up his cock, then put some lube on his fingers and slowly stuck it into my hole. I sat down on his dick, and it slid in pretty easily.

I pulled Michael's head up while I was riding his cock, so I could kiss him. I had wanted him to fuck me for so long and it was finally happening. His dick felt so good going in and out of my hole, and he fucked me like that for a good seven or eight minutes before I knew I wasn't going to be able to last any longer. I told him to grab my dick, and he started stroking it really fast. Within seconds, I was shooting my load on his chest with some going up to his chin. He gave his cock a few hard thrusts into my ass, and I knew he was cumming. He let out a loud moan, and then pulled his cock out and pulled the condom off so he could finish cumming on his chest. I leaned down and kissed him some more, and then we jumped in the shower.

When we walked back out into the living room, Thomas and Brandon were back on the couch. Brandon was sitting on the couch jerking off and Thomas was kneeling in front of him sucking on his balls. Thomas had obviously already gotten off, so now it was Brandon's turn. Without even thinking about it, I grabbed the bottle of lube and got Brandon's dick nice and went. I turned around and sat my ass down on it. His cock was smaller than Michael's, but it still felt pretty good. I bounced up and down on his dick while Thomas and Michael made out in front of me.

Brandon was grabbing onto my hips and rubbing his hands down my back, pushing me forward a bit. He said he was going to cum but said he couldn't cum in my ass. He pushed me up and off his cock, and just as he did his jizz shot straight up in the air. Some of it even got on my back. I quickly turned around and knelt down in front of him so he could jerk the rest of his load off on my face. Thomas came over and licked up some of the jizz. We turned the movie back on and finished it, and after that night, we never heard from either of them again.

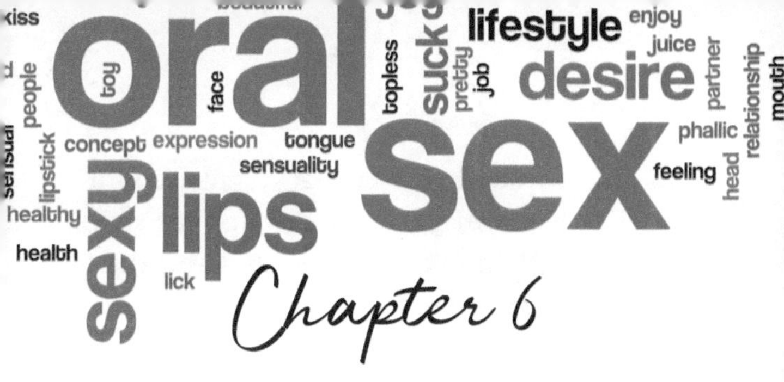

Chapter 6

CHARLIE & DANTE

I woke up the next morning pretty eager and excited for my session with Charlie and Dante. I was anxious to meet Dante, but also curious how the session was going to go, especially with Charlie's comment about my ass. I kind of felt like a teenager getting ready for a date and made sure I wore some nicer clothes and smelled super good and sexy.

I got to the office and made sure everything was nice and tidy, and about ten minutes later, Charlie walked in the front door followed by a gorgeous looking Greek man who was obviously Dante. His skin was sun-kissed, his hair was a glossy jet black, and I could practically see his six pack through his skin-tight shirt. I shook Charlie's hand and then introduced myself to Dante.

"Dante, it's so nice to meet you. I've been working with Charlie for a week now, and he's told me a lot about your relationship, as well as your sex life. My job here is to figure out what makes the both of you, shall I say, tick, and ensure you are able to maintain a strong and healthy relationship."

I told Dante that I was aware of their main issue—both of them being tops—and asked him to explain why he chose to perform in only that position.

"I've had a lot of boyfriends, and I used to consider myself to be pretty versatile," Dante told me. "I really didn't care what position I was fucking in, as long as I got to fuck and as long as I was able to cum. As I got older, something weird happened and I stopped being able to cum when I was bottoming, and I would have to wait for whoever was fucking me to cum so he could pull out and then just let me jerk off. Now don't get me wrong—the sex was always decent and what guy doesn't like jerking off—but it's just so much better when someone else is the cause of the explosion. So after dealing with this for a while, I just finally made the decision that I was going to be a top from here on out."

I thought that was an interesting point of view, and when I asked why he didn't try bottoming for Charlie, Dante said he just didn't want to even experience the disappointment of not cumming ever again. He said he was ALWAYS able to cum when he topped, so he just stuck with it.

I explained to both of them that during this session, they were each going to try bottoming. They both argued with me a little bit, but I ensure them that this was the only way we would be able to really diagnose what was actually going on. I told them that I would leave the room while this occurred, and they were to come get me from my other office when they were done so we could discuss.

Charlie quickly chimed in and said that he wanted me to stay. He said that he would feel better if I were there—for moral support. I didn't mind at all getting to stay and watch, so I quickly agreed.

Charlie got up off the couch and knelt down in front of Dante. He pulled his pants down while Dante took off his shirt. Charlie grabbed his cock and started sucking on it, and Dante rubbed his hands down his back and toward the top of his ass. I could see that Dante had a pretty thick cock, which might explain part of Charlie's hesitation in letting it go in.

Charlie sucked on Dante's cock for about five or six minutes, and then turned around and looked at me. At this point, I had my clipboard covering my own boner – it was impossible not to get hard watching this.

Charlie said, "Hey Doc, come join us." I quickly said no, but Charlie turned around and crawled over toward me, forcing himself in between my legs. He grabbed my clipboard and threw it across the room, smiling when he saw my hard cock turning my pants into a teepee.

I looked over at Dante, who was stroking his cock and smiling. Charlie started taking off my belt and unzipped my pants, reaching in and whipping my cock out through the opening. The moment his tongue touched the tip of penis sent my head back and my eyes rolling into the back of my head. His mouth was so warm and went, and he slowly licked the tip before sucking on just the head, and then devoured my entire rod.

He bobbed his head up and down rather slowly, taking every inch I had to offer. Then he started going faster before slowing down again.

For a minute, I completely forgot that Dante was even there, until he got up and walked over next to my chair, forcing his massive tool right into my face. Without hesitation, I grabbed onto his piece and he grabbed the back of my head and shoved his snake completely down my throat, making me really gag. I had one hand on Charlie's head as he bounced up and down, and another stroking on Dante's dick as it went in and out of my mouth.

We kept sucking on each other's cocks for several minutes before Dante got down on the ground next to Charlie to share mine. They each took a side of the shaft and were rubbing their lips and tongues up and down. One would put my entire piece in their mouth while the other would suck on my balls and go down toward my hole, and then they'd switch positions. After a few minutes, I told them it was time for one of them to bottom.

Charlie said that he'd go first but that he wanted me to fuck him instead of Dante, to loosen him up a bit. I took off my shirt while Charlie pulled off the rest of my pants, and we moved over to the couch. I sat down and lubed up my cock, and then poured some lube on my finger to get Charlie's hole nice and wet. Dante sat down next to me and started stroking my cock while I was getting Charlie ready.

Charlie straddled me and slowly started sitting down until the head of my penis was touching his hole. I could tell he was nervous and hesitant, and I told him that he had full control over this. He lowered his ass a little more, and I could feel just how tight his hole was as my head entered it. He let out a scream, and I even saw a tear fall from his eye. Holy fuck, his hole felt so good, even with just the tip in. It was almost like a vacuum.

Dante was sitting back and stroking his cock in pure excitement. Charlie lowered himself a little more, and with each inch of my dick that disappeared inside of him, he would take a minute to breathe and let his hold expand.

It took a few minutes, but my cock had finally disappeared in his ass, and he just sat there for a minute taking a bit of a breather. As ready as I was to just start pounding away at his ass, I also needed to be a professional and let him control this.

He slowly raised his ass up, and then brought it back down on my member even more slowly. After a few minutes of this I could tell he was starting to get the hang of it, and he started going faster and faster. Dante leaned over and started sucking on Charlie's cock while he was riding me, and the moans and sounds coming out of his mouth were unlike any other. This was like popping a guy's cherry, and it was fucking amazing.

After a few minutes, Charlie said that it was Dante's turn. Charlie got off my cock and stood up, and Dante moved over and started to stradddle me. Charlie quickly said, "Umm, no. I'm fucking you. Not the doc." So, Dante leaned over me and started kissing me, getting on all fours and inviting Charlie to stick his dick in his ass. Charlie bent down and stuck his tongue in Dante's ass, getting it nice and wet while he was lubing up his own cock. Dante was a pretty good kisser and put his head down and started sucking on my cock.

Charlie was very slow and gentle in putting his hard cock into Dante's ass, and Dante didn't even seem to flinch or notice. I guess that was no surprise, though. Dante wasn't afraid of the pain; he was just afraid of not cumming. Once Charlie had his piece completely engulfed by Dante's hole, he grabbed his hips and immediately started rough fucking him. Dante was still sucking on my dick, so his moans had a mouthful in them.

I pulled Dante's head up from sucking on my dick and slid down off the couch in front of him. I wanted to make sure that this was a good "first" experience for him, so I slid in front of him and started sucking on his cock. Who in the world wouldn't cum from getting fucked and sucked at the same time? He was still on all fours and using the couch to hold him up, so I had pretty easy access to his massive dick. I let that entire thing go back into my mouth and stroked and sucked it until I could feel it start throbbing.

Dante let out a loud moan and said, "I'm going to blow!" Charlie kept pounding away, and I kept sucking on it. He blew such a huge load in my mouth that I couldn't even swallow all of it—most of it came exploding out of my mouth. I kept going, though, because I wanted to make sure that he had the best orgasm *we* could give him. To my surprise, he let Charlie continue fucking him for a few minutes while I wiped my face off. I noticed that Dante's cock was still rock hard, so I told them they needed to switch positions.

I leaned over the side of the couch and told Charlie to come up behind me and start fucking me, and then Dante got behind him. Charlie put his dick in me but waited to start thrusting until Dante was inside of him. I could feel the moment that Dante shoved his cock in Charlie's hole because Charlies' dick inside of me felt like it grew the same moment.

Charlie, being in the middle, did most of the motion, and was letting out some pretty loud sounds. I couldn't help but moan myself because his cock in my hole felt pretty amazing. I moved forward so that Charlie's dick would slide out of my hole so that the two of them could fuck for a little bit.

Dante pushed Charlie's head down into the couch, grabbed his hips and started thrusting his cock in and out of his hole. I stood on the side, watching and stroking my cock. Seeing the two of them go at it was like seeing two models walk the runway. This was possibly the hottest thing I had ever experienced. After a few minutes, Charlie looked at me and motioned for me to come back. He said he was getting close to cumming and wanted to cum in my hole.

I got back on the edge of the couch, this time on my back, and let Charlie lift my legs above his shoulders and slide his wet member back inside of me. Dante immediately started pounding away, and not even twenty seconds later, Charlie busted out, "I'm gonna nut!" Dante started pounding harder, and as soon as that milk started shooting out of Charlie's dick, I could feel my hole getting flooded. Charlie gave a few more good pumps inside of me, and then I head Dante say, "I'm gonna blow again." I was shocked because I didn't think he was going to cum again, but then again, he was a Greek God.

Dante gave Charlie's hole a few more good thrusts and then let out a massive scream. At the same time, I saw Charlie's body shake as his hole was filled with Dante's load. Dante kept pumping it inside of him until he knew his cock was completely drained, and then pulled his dick out. He came around Charlie and knelt down in front of me and said, "Your turn."

His cock was still covered in cum, and he shoved it right inside my hole and started pounding away. How the fuck was this guy able to maintain an erection after blowing twice? Charlie came over and started stroking my cock, and I couldn't even give warning when I shot my load straight up and over my head. Dante pulled his dick out and Charlie bent down to suck the rest of the cum off of it, and then started licking all the cum off my chest.

We all got up and got dressed, and I told them that I felt like this was a very successful session, but that I still wanted them to come back for periodic follow-up sessions to ensure the successes remained. They both gave me a kiss on the cheek as they left, and I just sat down in my chair, kind of wondering what the fuck just happened.

The next day, when I came into the office, I noticed I had new messages for appointment requests. By the time I had gotten through all the requests, I had 24 new patients booked.

Obviously, Charlie and Dante had spread the word about the success of our sessions, and business was about to be booming.

As I closed out my messaging system, I heard the bell at the front door ring. This skinny boy walked in and asked if he could make an appointment. I didn't think I'd have walk-ins, but I asked him to briefly describe what he was going through. He told me he had met a guy that he was in love with, but both of them were bottoms, and it was really impacting their sex life.

"So, you're saying that you're only a bottom?" I asked him.

At that moment, I already knew where my sessions with this boy would lead.

Author Bio

Grayson Ace has had his fair share of sexcapades, and figured why not write about them? Recently divorced, he is re-discovering himself (and plenty of hot men) and creating many new sexy adventures along the way. If you like what you see, please leave a review, and you never know....you may end up in one of the stories!

GraysonAce.com
Facebook: Grayson Ace
Instagram: graysonaceofficial
Twitter: @GraysonAce1

More Books From Grayson Ace

How I Got Here
First Year Out of the Closet
You're Only a Top?
You're Only a Bottom?
I Think I'm a Serial Swiper